Slider's Pet

ALL ABOUT NATURE

Written by Kirsten Hall

Illustrated by Bev Luedecke

children's press®

A Division of Scholastic Inc.
New York Toronto London Auckland Sydney
Mexico City New Delhi Hong Kong
Danbury, Connecticut

About the Author

Kirsten Hall, formerly an early-childhood teacher,
is a children's book editor in New York City. She has been
writing books for children since she was thirteen years old
and now has over sixty titles in print.

About the Illustrator

Bev Luedecke enjoys life and nature in Colorado.
Her sparkling personality and artistic flair are reflected in her
creation of Beastieville, a world filled with lovable Beasties
that are sure to delight children of all ages.

Library of Congress Cataloging-in-Publication Data

Hall, Kirsten.
  Slider's pet : all about nature / written by Kirsten Hall; illustrated by Bev Luedecke.
    p. cm. — (Beastieville)
  Summary: Slider has a new pet chipmunk, but the other Beasties explain why wild animals should be set free.
  ISBN 0-516-22898-6 (lib. bdg.)   0-516-25522-3 (pbk.)
  [1. Chipmunks as pets—Fiction. 2. Wild animals as pets—Fiction. 3. Pets—Fiction. 4. Stories in rhyme.]
I. Luedecke, Bev, ill. II. Title.
  PZ8.3.H146Sli 2004
  [E]—dc22
                                                                    2004000123

Text © 2004 Nancy Hall, Inc. Illustrations © 2004 Bev Luedecke. All rights reserved.
Published in 2004 by Children's Press, an imprint of Scholastic Library Publishing.
Printed in the United States of America. Developed by Nancy Hall, Inc.

1 2 3 4 5 6 7 8 9 10 R 13 12 11 10 09 08 07 06 05 04

A NOTE TO PARENTS AND TEACHERS

Welcome to the world of the Beasties, where learning is FUN. In each of the charming stories in this series, the Beasties deal with character traits that every child can identify with. Each story reinforces appropriate concept skills for kindergartners and first graders, while simultaneously encouraging problem-solving skills. Following are just a few of the ways that you can help children get the most from this delightful series.

Stories to be read and enjoyed

Encourage children to read the stories aloud. The rhyming verses make them fun to read. Then ask them to think about alternate solutions to some of the problems that the Beasties have faced or to imagine alternative endings. Invite children to think about what they would have done if they were in the story and to recall similar things that have happened to them.

Activities reinforce the learning experience

The activities at the end of the books offer a way for children to put their new skills to work. They complement the story and are designed to help children develop specific skills and build confidence. Use these activities to reinforce skills. But don't stop there. Encourage children to find ways to build on these skills during the course of the day.

Learning opportunities are everywhere

Use this book as a starting point for talking about how we use reading skills or math or social studies concepts in everyday life. When we search for a phone number in the telephone book and scan names in alphabetical order or check a list, we are using reading skills. When we keep score at a baseball game or divide a class into even-numbered teams, we are using math.

The more you can help children see that the skills they are learning in school really do have a place in everyday life, the more they will think of learning as something that is part of their lives, not as a chore to be borne. Plus you will be sending the important message that learning is fun.

Madeline Boskey Olsen, Ph.D.
Developmental Psychologist

Bee-Bop

Puddles

Slider

Wilbur

Pip & Zip

Flippet

Pooky

Mr. Rigby

We're the Beasties

Smudge

Toggles

It is fall in Beastieville.
Leaves are falling. Some are red.

It will soon be wintertime.
Slider stays warm in his bed.

He has found himself a pet.
He likes his new pet a lot.

Zip and Pip stop by to see.
"Do you like the pet I got?"

"Chipmunks are not pets," says Zip.
"You must let that chipmunk go!"

"Chipmunks can not live inside?
Is that true? I did not know!"

"I thought he would like it here!
This is better than a tree."

Zip and Pip just shake their heads.
"It is best to set him free."

"Chipmunks need to be outside.
That is where they like to play.

They play with their chipmunk friends.
They need space to run all day."

"If he stays, I'll give him food.
What do chipmunks like to eat?"

Pooky knows what chipmunks like.
"How about a berry treat?"

Bee-Bop joins his friends outside.
"Chipmunks love to eat nuts, too!"

Bee-Bop points down at the ground.
"He does not need help from you!"

Slider asks, "Where will he live?
Soon it will get cold out here!"

Slider says, "He might get sick!
What will he do then? Oh, dear!"

"He will make himself a home!"
Bee-Bop knows just what to say.

"He will gather leaves and sticks.
Slider, he will be okay!"

Here comes Toggles. "Is it big?"
Here comes Flippet. "Is it small?"

Wilbur does not care one bit.
"I do not like pets at all."

Puddles comes to join her friends.
Mr. Rigby comes out, too.

"Slider, where is your new pet?
Do you have it here with you?"

Smudge asks Slider, "What is wrong?
Why is your pet running free?"

Slider says, "I let him go.
He does not belong to me!"

A NEW HOME

1. How many leaves is the chipmunk using to make his new home?

2. How many sticks has the chipmunk found?

3. How many Beasties are watching the chipmunk build his home?

SOUNDS LIKE...

"Blue" is a word that sounds like "new." Can you think of any other words that sound like "new"?

HAVING A PET

Having a pet is a big job.

1. What kinds of animals make good pets?

2. How do you take care of a pet?

3. Why don't wild animals make good pets?

WORD LIST

a	eat	in	pet	then
about	fall	inside	pets	they
all	falling	is	Pip	this
and	Flippet	it	play	thought
are	food	join	points	to
asks	found	joins	Pooky	Toggles
at	free	just	Puddles	too
be	friends	know	red	treat
Beastieville	from	knows	Rigby	tree
bed	gather	leaves	run	true
Bee-Bop	get	let	running	warm
belong	give	like	say	what
berry	go	likes	says	where
best	got	live	see	why
better	ground	lot	set	Wilbur
big	has	love	shake	will
bit	have	make	sick	wintertime
by	he	me	Slider	with
can	heads	might	small	would
care	help	Mr.	Smudge	wrong
chipmunk	her	must	some	you
chipmunks	here	need	soon	your
cold	him	new	space	Zip
comes	himself	not	stays	
day	his	nuts	sticks	
dear	home	oh	stop	
did	how	okay	than	
do	I	one	that	
does	if	out	the	
down	I'll	outside	their	